Surviving
Brick
Johnson

Surviving
Brick
Johnson

by **LAURIE MYERS**

illustrated by **DAN YACCARINO**

Clarion Books ▪ New York

For Barnwell and Jean Myers
—L.M.

Clarion Books
a Houghton Mifflin Company imprint
215 Park Avenue South, New York, NY 10003

Text copyright © 2000 by Laurie Myers
Illustrations copyright © 2000 by Dan Yaccarino

The illustrations were executed in gouache.
The text was set in 14-point Century ITC Book.

www.hmco.com/trade

Printed in Shenzhen, China

SURVIVING BRICK JOHNSON by Laurie Myers, illustrated by Dan Yaccarino.
Text copyright © 2000 by Laurie Myers. Illustrations copyright © 2000 by Dan Yaccarino.
Reprinted by arrangement with Clarion Books, an imprint of
Houghton Mifflin Harcourt Publishing Company. All rights reserved.

Library of Congress Cataloging-in-Publication Data
Myers, Laurie.
Surviving Brick Johnson / Laurie Myers ; pictures by Dan Yaccarino.
p. cm.
Summary: Afraid of getting maimed for making fun of Brick, the husky new kid in his fifth-
grade class, Alex decides that even his baseball collection will not protect him, so he signs up for
karate class despite his little brother's reassurances that Brick is not a bully.
ISBN 0-395-98031-3
[1. Schools–Fiction. 2. Brothers–Fiction. 3. Conduct of life–Fiction.]
I. Yaccarino, Dan, ill. II. Title.

PZ7.M9873 Su 2000
[Fic]–dc21   00-024309

0413/13000122
ISBN 978-0-325-04849-9

18 17 16 15 14 13 RRD 1 2 3 4 5 6

Contents

chapter 1

A Sleek Fighting Machine

Alex yanked open his desk drawer with the urgency of a boy about to die. His baseball cards fell to the floor unnoticed. Papers flew everywhere. He *had* to find that flyer. His very life depended on it. His teacher had passed it out on the first day of school, and he had brought it home and tossed it into his desk. He *knew* he had.

Alex spotted the paper. He grabbed it and read carefully.

Karate classes for Lakeside Elementary students
Tuesday, September 8 at 7:00 p.m.
Call the YMCA to register

Tuesday. Alex breathed a sigh of relief.

Today was Tuesday. He wasn't late.

He studied the picture at the bottom of the page. It showed a muscular man poised for a fight. The caption under the picture read, "A Sleek Fighting Machine."

Perfect!

A sleek fighting machine was exactly what Alex needed to be if he was going to survive fifth grade and Brick Johnson. They had only been in school for two weeks and already Brick was after him.

They had been in the lunchroom. Everyone was doing imitations.

"What's up, Doc?" Megan had said, pushing out her front teeth.

"Bugs Bunny!" everyone yelled.

"Beep, beep," said tall, skinny Tom in a high, squeaky voice.

"Road Runner!" everyone yelled.

Alex wasn't sure what made him do it, but he pulled his shoulders back, squared his body, stiffened his arms at his side and said, "I'm big and square. The third little pig made a house out of me." He patted his middle.

"Brick Johnson!" everyone yelled, then laughed.

Alex puffed out his chest for another laugh. That's when he saw Brick staring at him. Brick's lips formed a straight line that resembled a grin. Alex had seen that look on the nature channel a million times. It wasn't a grin. It was the look of a wild animal right before a kill.

Brick lumbered over to the table, and stood directly across from Alex. His baseball cap was pulled low on his head. His shirttail hung out on one side. He looked big and mean.

Alex's hand still rested on his abdomen, but not as a joke anymore. He felt sick. He was glad the table stood between Brick and him. Brick leaned over and placed both hands on the table.

"At my other school a boy did an imitation of me and . . ."

At that moment Coach Bonner, the P.E. teacher, walked by.

"Stay at your own table during lunch," he said.

Brick turned and walked back to his table.

After a moment of silence, everyone began to breathe again.

"He's so big," Susan said.

"And he always wears that Braves hat," Megan added.

"Only when they win. If they lose, he wears the opposing team's hat," Susan said.

Normally that would have been of interest to Alex. Not now.

"What do you think Brick did to that boy who imitated him?" Tom asked.

Alex was silent. With somebody named Brick, the possibilities were limitless.

"More importantly, what's he gonna do to *you*?" Megan asked.

"Maybe he's going to maim you," Susan Green said.

"Where did you get that?" Tom asked.

"It's one of our words for this week. Haven't you done the vocabulary unit?"

Alex had not done the vocabulary unit, so as

soon as he got home, he looked up "maim" in the dictionary.

maim. 1. to cause serious physical injury

Yep. That made sense. Brick did want to cause him serious physical injury. The second and third definitions were worse.

maim. 2. to disable or make defective

maim. 3. to deprive a person of a limb or member of the body

Alex's muscles tensed. He didn't want to be defective, and he certainly didn't want to lose a member of his body. He wiggled his fingers to reassure himself of their vitality.

It was amazing how your life could change. Only a few weeks ago, he had been having the best summer of his life. He had spent most of the time organizing his baseball cards. First, he organized them according to teams. Then, he reorganized them according to positions. Occasionally, he would pull out his favorite players, handling them carefully so he wouldn't accidentally "maim" them.

Alex carried the dictionary into the kitchen, where his mother was cooking dinner.

"Mom, exactly how important are the second and third definitions of a word?"

"It depends on the word."

That was the answer Alex hated most. *It depends*. Was he going to get a serious physical injury or be deprived of a limb? *It depends*.

Brick would know all the possible definitions for maim. After all, dentists knew dental words, and mechanics knew car words. But which definition did Brick have in mind: the first, second, or third definition?

Suddenly, Alex grew cold. Maybe Brick was planning on all three! He grabbed the phone and dialed the YMCA.

chapter 2

The Solution to World War

"I want each person to tell the best—and the worst—thing that happened to them today," Alex's mother said at dinner.

Alex wondered if he should tell about Brick. He looked around the table. Liz, his sister, was carefully picking sesame seeds off her roll. She would not understand. She was too wrapped up in her new life in middle school.

His brother, Bob, was shoveling mashed potatoes into his mouth. He was only in first grade. What did he know of real danger?

Alex's mother sat across from him, carefully cutting Bob's meat into small pieces. She worked in the emergency room at the hospital.

She wouldn't consider maiming very serious.

"Bob, what was your worst thing today?" Mrs. Wilson said, pulling the last piece of meat off the fork.

"Somebody spit on me," Bob said.

"Spit on you! That's gross," Liz said. She gave her roll a final inspection and took a bite.

Spitting didn't sound so bad to Alex. He would trade spitting for maiming any day. In fact, spitting

was a wonderful alternative to maiming. Starting in first grade, kids should be taught to spit. When a person got mad, he could simply spit on the other person. No one would ever get hurt. Even presidents of countries could spit. When men joined the army, they would be issued a raincoat.

"I got to be line leader. That was the good thing," Bob said.

"We need line leaders at middle school," Liz said. "Everything is more complicated over there."

"Liz, what was your best thing?" Mrs. Wilson asked.

"Andrew Marshall asked me out."

"And your worst thing?" Alex asked, wondering if she could top Brick Johnson.

"Andrew Marshall asked me out."

If good and bad were the same in middle school, then things were definitely more complicated. At least in Alex's life bad things were bad, and good things were good. His problem: Brick Johnson was going to maim him—nothing confusing about that. It was definitely bad.

"Alex, what about you?" his mother asked.

"A boy at school is going to maim me," he blurted out.

"What's maim?" Bob asked.

"To cause serious physical injury," Alex said solemnly.

"Did someone actually threaten to maim you?" Mrs. Wilson said.

"Well, not exactly."

"Did he threaten to beat you up?" Liz asked.

"No."

"Spit on you?" Bob asked.

"No."

"Then what exactly did he say?" Mrs. Wilson asked. Alex could feel their expectations build.

"He didn't actually *say* what he was going to do," Alex admitted.

Mrs. Wilson gave him a look that said she was not impressed.

"If he does do something, he'll get timeout," Bob said. "That's what happened to Harriet when she spit on me."

"This boy needs timeout for the rest of his life," Alex said.

"That's called jail," Liz said.

Alex imagined himself lying on the ground while the police carted Brick off to jail.

"Timeout for the rest of your life, Buddy," one policeman would say.

His partner would glance back at Alex. "It's too late for that poor guy. Too bad he wasn't a sleek fighting machine. "

Alex felt hopeful. Walt, the instructor, had been real nice on the phone. He had suggested that Alex come early and observe one of the classes.

Liz said, "There is one solution: Never be alone with him. He probably won't do anything to you in front of other people, especially not a teacher."

"Yeah, hang around the teacher," Bob said enthusiastically.

Alex imagined himself with the teachers, eating at their lunch table, hanging out at their recess gathering. It would be a dismal existence, but maybe better than no existence at all.

"I recommend a peaceful solution," his mother said. "Go and talk to this boy. Sometimes bullies are not as bad as they appear."

"Yeah. And sometimes they're worse," Liz said. She laughed, then added, "Just in case something does happen, make out a will and leave me your baseball card collection. I told Andrew Marshall about it and he said it was worth some money."

"Liz," Mrs. Wilson said, "you are not being helpful."

"Alex, what was your good thing?" Bob asked.

Alex thought for a moment. "I have two good things. One, I'm going to find a Ted Williams baseball card. Two, I'm starting karate classes tonight."

"Karate classes? Tonight?" Mrs. Wilson said. Her fork hovered in front of her mouth.

"Yes. It's a special class for Lakeside students. I already called, and they have plenty of room."

Mrs. Wilson studied her son's face.

"Mom, it will be good exercise. You're always saying I need more exercise."

"That's true," she said slowly. "Where are the classes held?"

"At the YMCA on Evans Road. It's not that far. I can ride my bike."

"Mom, you should be glad he's doing something besides sitting around shuffling baseball cards," Liz said.

Mrs. Wilson nodded. "Okay."

Liz picked up her plate and carried it to the sink. "Don't forget that will," she added.

Alex picked up his plate and headed for the sink, too. If things went well tonight, he wouldn't need a will.

chapter 3

Respect

Mirrors covered two walls of the large room, and a thick blue mat covered the floor. The other two walls were covered with wise sayings like "Make your enemy your friend" and "Welcome the chance to learn about others."

Alex focused on the students scattered around the room. They wore clean white uniforms and different colored belts: some white, some yellow, still others green. The instructor, who was probably Walt, wore a black belt with gold stripes on the end.

The students paired off and quietly circled each other, never letting their eyes leave their opponent. Alex recognized this stalking behavior. It occurred right before an animal turned into a sleek fighting machine.

Hopefully, Alex would soon be a sleek fighting machine. He looked in the mirror that covered the wall. He was already sleek. Some people in school called him puny. He preferred sleek. If he could just add "fighting machine" to the description, then everything would be perfect.

Alex flexed his arm and watched in the mirror as a small lump appeared. It looked like a Ping-Pong ball. What he wanted was a baseball.

As the class ended, the students lined up to face the instructor.

"Respect!" the students yelled together as they began reciting the creed.

Alex smiled. Respect was exactly what he wanted.

The students bowed to the instructor. He returned their bow and then made his way over to Alex.

He extended his hand. His grip was firm. "Hi. I'm Walt. You must be Alex. I like your enthusiasm. Let's get started."

"Sure," Alex said eagerly. He followed Walt

to the corner of the room where a large red punching bag hung from the ceiling.

"First we bow. It shows we respect each other," Walt said.

Alex bowed deeply. It felt good. He decided immediately that everyone should bow. Teachers and students should bow before class. Friends should bow before a Monopoly game. There was one exception. Brick Johnson. You should never bow to Brick. He might konk you on the back of the head, and your last view of the world would be the ground.

"Let's start with some stretching exercises."

Walt sat on the floor with one leg bent and the other straight. He reached for his toe and began a routine. Alex copied each exercise.

Walt stood and faced the bag. "Okay, let's try a round kick. Look at the way I position my body. Notice how my heel is turned in."

Alex turned his heel in. He wobbled slightly. It wasn't quite as easy as it looked.

"Like this," Walt said.

Alex repositioned his feet and kept his balance.

"Good. Now swing your leg up and around, like this."

Walt swung his leg up and jabbed the bag. It vibrated with a *smack*. Walt stilled the bag.

"Now you try it."

Alex took his position. He swung his leg up and around. His foot made a soft slap against the bag.

"Nice kick and good balance. Do it a few more times."

"One sleek fighting machine coming up," Alex thought. This was going to be easy.

As Alex practiced his round kick, Walt asked,

"What did you like best about the class you observed?"

"Respect," Alex blurted out. His answer surprised him.

Walt smiled. "To be respected, you must first show respect. Fighting is the easy part of karate. Respect and self-control are the difficult parts."

Alex didn't believe that for a moment. Besides, what was important right now was a good strong round kick. That's what would save him from Brick. Alex kicked the bag again.

At the end of the lesson Walt gave Alex a white uniform and belt.

"This is your gi. Keep it neat and clean. But never wash your belt. Every drop of sweat and hard work should show on your belt. Wear your gi tomorrow when you come to class."

Alex took the gi and tucked it under his arm. He bowed deeply, and Walt returned the bow.

When Alex stepped outside into the cool evening air, he felt a surge of confidence. He kicked the air. "Take that, Brick!" he yelled loudly.

chapter 4

The Hundred-Year-Old Man

"Is that boy in your class going to get you today?" Bob asked as they rode the bus to school.

"No," Alex said, with more confidence than he felt.

Last night he had felt sure of himself. This morning he had awakened with one word etched in his mind. *Run*.

"The guy's pretty big. I think I can outrun him," Alex said.

Running was easy. Alex could run all day if necessary, ducking in and out of hallways, dashing up and down stairs. It was a cowardly plan, but that didn't matter. Survival was what mattered.

"Do you have baseball players with you?" Bob asked.

Alex smiled. He always kept a few baseball cards with him. He felt more confident when he had the right players with him. They inspired him.

He pulled two cards out of his pocket and formed them into a fan for Bob to see. He pointed to the first card. "This is Barry Bonds. He's fast."

Speed was important today. Brick was probably slow, but Alex couldn't count on that. He needed to be fast.

"This is Mike Piazza. He's a catcher. He's not fast, but he's alert. He has to be ready for any pitch, especially a wild pitch."

Alex would need to be alert, too. Brick could be hiding anywhere: behind a water fountain, in the restroom, in a classroom doorway. Alex would have to be alert to all the possibilities.

"Mike Piazza is also a powerful hitter," he added, hoping he wouldn't need that skill.

Alex passed the cards to Bob. "What I need is the card of a really special, truly great player."

"Ted Williams?" Bob asked.

"Exactly! Ted Williams would be perfect. He

was the last player to bat .400. He hit 521 home runs. He had incredible statistics, even though he missed five seasons. And he was a Marine, too."

"Wow. Can you get a Ted Williams card?"

"I don't know. I saw one on the Internet last night, but it would take too long. I need the card now. I'm going to ask around school today. I might be able to trade for one."

"I hope you get it," Bob said. Then he sighed. "I

wish I had somebody to help me with Harriet."

Suddenly, his face brightened. "Maybe the hundred-year-old man can help."

"Who?" Alex asked.

"A one-hundred-year-old man is visiting our class today. We get to ask him questions about his life."

Alex imagined himself as a hundred-year-old man being interviewed by a reporter.

"Sir, what has helped you live so long?" the reporter asked.

The one-hundred-year-old Alex answered, "Baseball cards. Let me tell you about the time Mike Piazza and Barry Bonds saved my life."

"But I don't really think the hundred-year-old man can help," Bob continued. "Harriet will just spit on him, too."

"Okay, here's a plan," said Alex. "Tell Harriet that if she spits on you, then you'll spit on her. Show her you mean business. Get a big spit glob on your lips. Like this."

Bob watched intently, then ran his tongue around the inside of his mouth, trying to collect saliva. A small drop rolled over his lip and fell onto his jacket.

"It won't stay," he complained.

"Get some air in your spit. That makes it stick together," Alex said.

Bob's cheeks sounded like suction cups as he worked on his spit glob. Finally, a large airy spit-ball formed and sat poised on his bottom lip.

"Ready to launch," Alex said.

Bob swallowed and smiled. "Now *I* have a plan for Harriet, and *you* have a plan for. . . . What's his name?"

"Who?"

"The boy who's going to get you."

"Brick Johnson."

Bob's face dropped. "Brick Johnson?"

"Yeah. Do you know him?"

"Yes, and he would never hurt you." Bob sounded personally offended.

"What makes you say that?"

"Brick Johnson is nice," Bob said.

"How do you know?"

"He comes to our class and reads us stories."

Alex had a vague memory of Mrs. Gilstrap, his teacher, asking for volunteers to read to the younger classes. He hadn't given it a second thought.

Bob started laughing. "You should hear Brick do the dog's voice."

Alex stared at his brother, whose face was bright.

"Brick is a Braves fan, too," Bob said enthusiastically. "He wears their cap when they win."

"I know," Alex mumbled.

Alex tried to process this new information about Brick. It didn't fit his picture of Brick—a big mean bully, ready to maim an innocent fellow fifth grader. He tried to imagine Brick doing funny dog imitations. Impossible.

The bus stopped.

"Have a nice day," the driver called.

Alex looked out the window. His pulse quickened. Somewhere inside that school was Brick Johnson, and he probably wasn't doing funny dog imitations.

chapter 5

Stealing Home

As Alex moved through the crowded hallway, his heart was pounding. He couldn't believe how nervous he felt. He should be calm. After all, he had Barry Bonds and Mike Piazza with him. Plus he was off to a great start in karate. Tonight he could finish his round kick, and maybe tomorrow he would be ready to take on Brick.

Alex peered around the corner to the cafeteria. No sign of a Braves cap. The Braves had won last night, so Brick would be wearing their cap. Maybe Brick was out sick today.

Alex relaxed a little as he headed for class. Only one more turn and he would be in his classroom, safely in the presence of the teacher. He glanced over his shoulder as he made the last turn.

Bam! A large object stopped him.

Brick!

He wasn't sick. In fact, he had never looked healthier.

Alex jumped back, whirled around, and headed in the opposite direction.

"Hey," Brick said.

"Steal second!" Alex yelled to himself. He raced down the hall.

Everything went by in a blur. In two steps he was at the door to the playground. He pushed open the door, darted around the corner, and collapsed against the wall.

Safe at second.

Alex leaned there, sucking in air. His plan had worked. That was the good news. The bad news: he still needed to get to class. He didn't have much time. He took a deep breath.

"Steal third," he commanded.

He sprang away from the wall and circled the school to the front door. He peered in. The halls were almost empty now. He pushed open the door and ran for his classroom. He raced past the first-grade rooms. Past the second-grade rooms. One more turn. Alex rounded the corner and . . .

Bam! A large object stopped him.

Mr. Watkins, the principal!

Mr. Watkins grabbed Alex by the shoulders. "Hey, slow down."

Alex was actually glad to see Mr. Watkins. He was bigger than Brick, but not nearly as bad. He might give Alex detention, but at least he wouldn't maim him.

Safe at third.

"You know the rule about running in the halls," Mr. Watkins said, releasing Alex.

"Yes, sir," Alex said.

"Maybe lunch detention will help you remember that rule."

"Yes, sir," Alex said, trying not to show his relief.

Lunch detention was perfect! You had to sit with a teacher for the entire lunch period. That was exactly what Liz and Bob had suggested.

"Now go on to class and no more running," Mr. Watkins said.

"Yes, sir," Alex said.

He walked into his classroom.

Safe at home.

chapter 6

First-Grade Comedian

Out of the corner of his eye, Alex could see Brick on the other side of the room, listening to Mrs. Gilstrap read the morning announcements.

"The YMCA karate class started last night. There is still room if anyone is interested. It's at seven o'clock tonight at the Y," she said.

Alex hoped no one came. He wanted to be the only "sleek fighting machine" in his class. He imagined himself doing a powerful round kick and flattening Brick.

Suddenly, "Make your enemy your friend" popped into his head. That phrase sounded good, but it was probably one of those things that people said but didn't really mean. On the other hand, people at the karate studio took things seriously.

Alex made a mental note to ask Walt about it.

At the end of the announcements Mrs. Gilstrap said, "Brick, it's time to visit Mrs. Kendricks's class."

Mrs. Kendricks? That was Bob's teacher!

Alex sat up straighter. He watched Brick root around in his desk. Brick pulled out two picture books. One was about a dog that had a secret nightlife that his master didn't know about. Alex was familiar with the book. He had read it several times and liked it. The other book was about a baseball player.

Brick turned to leave the classroom, and Alex quickly looked away.

"I want the rest of you to finish the math problems on the board," Mrs. Gilstrap said.

Alex started the problems but only finished one. He kept thinking about Brick. Brick had been new in their school last year, so Alex didn't know that much about him. He certainly didn't know about the books or the dog imitations. Suddenly, Alex was overwhelmed with curiosity. His hand shot into the air.

"Yes, Alex," Mrs. Gilstrap said.

"I forgot to give my brother something this morning. Can I take it to him?"

Mrs. Gilstrap glanced at her watch. "Yes, but finish copying the assignments first."

Alex copied the assignments quickly. Before leaving the room he pulled something out of his pocket and wrapped it in a blank sheet of paper.

As he hurried toward the first-grade hall, Alex realized his actions made no sense. His plan had been to avoid Brick Johnson, and now he was following him. He was behaving exactly like those television characters who irritated him by doing the exact opposite of what they should do. They would hear a scary noise in the attic or basement and then, instead of running away, go investigate, slowly creeping toward what was obviously danger.

The door to Bob's classroom was closed. Alex peered through the window. Brick sat in the middle of a circle of first graders. His face was scrunched up into a million wrinkles as he read from a book. He turned the page and his face transformed into a dopey look. His hand made a pawing motion. The first graders howled. Alex found himself smiling. He pressed his ear to the door to hear what Brick was saying.

Suddenly, the door opened and Alex stumbled in.

"Can I help you?" Mrs. Kendricks asked.

The story stopped, and the first graders stared at Alex.

Bob waved vigorously and yelled, "That's my brother. Alex, Brick is reading the dog book. Come listen."

Brick looked puzzled or maybe embarrassed. Alex wasn't sure which.

"I have something for Bob," Alex said to Mrs. Kendricks.

"Bob, your brother is just delivering something. He can't stay," the teacher said.

Alex handed Bob the piece of paper. Bob peeked inside. His face lit up, and he gave Alex a thumbs-up.

On the way back to class Alex thought about Brick. He didn't look like a bully. He looked more like a . . . a . . . Alex hunted for the right word. He remembered the laughing first graders. A comedian, that was it—Brick looked like a comedian. He shouldn't be running from a comedian.

On the other hand, this particular comedian was planning to maim him.

Alex thought back to the lunchroom incident. Brick had not actually used the word "maim." What was it he had said? "At my other school a boy did an imitation of me and . . ."

And what? Alex wondered. ". . . and I kicked him." ". . . and I punched him." Or maybe, ". . . and *I* did an imitation of *him*." That was the best one of all. It would be great if Brick would imitate Alex. He smiled at the thought of Brick trying to make himself small.

All this was wishful thinking, he realized. Brick was planning to maim him. Fortunately, he had a simple three-part plan. Part one: Survive today. Part two: Perfect his round kick. Part three: Use his round kick to flatten Brick.

chapter 7

The Deadly Dictionary

Alex crouched between the shelves of nonfiction. If he made it through library period, part one of his plan would be complete.

Books about sharks, tigers, and other man-eating animals surrounded him. Alex almost expected to see Brick's name on one of the books.

"He's coming," someone whispered into the shelves. He sounded excited.

Alex crawled past the 600s and 700s. He stopped at the end of the row beside the 900s, the history books.

"Oh, hi, Brick," he heard someone say loudly. It sounded close.

Alex crawled some more. He started around to

the next aisle when a shoe stepped in and blocked his path.

No. It wasn't a shoe. It was a boot.

Alex froze.

The boot was too big for a normal student, and too dirty for a teacher. Only one person in the school would wear a boot that big and that dirty.

Brick Johnson!

In his fastest library walk, Alex hurried down the aisle to the reference section. Mrs. White was sitting

quietly at the desk, checking out books. Alex thought about throwing himself at her and screaming, "Save me!" but he resisted the urge. He couldn't do that in front of everyone in the library. He passed Mrs. White and hid in the biographies.

Brick entered the reference section and stopped.

Alex watched.

Why would he stop? Maybe he had decided it was too dangerous to maim someone in the library. After all, Mrs. White was right there.

Brick began inspecting the reference books.

Maybe he needs to look up something, Alex thought hopefully.

Brick pulled the largest dictionary off the shelf. Alex laughed softly. That dictionary probably had twenty definitions for maim.

Color drained from Alex's face as the truth struck him. Brick didn't want the dictionary as a reference. He wanted it . . . as a weapon!

Alex retreated quickly.

"Help," he said weakly, hoping the brave characters in the biographies would somehow jump out to help him.

Brick moved toward Alex.

"Where is the big dictionary?" Alex heard someone ask loudly.

Brick stopped. He was so close he could have heaved the dictionary and flattened Alex.

"I don't know. It was here a minute ago," Mrs. White said, looking around. "Oh, there it is. Clarence," she called.

Brick flinched when he heard his real name.

"Please leave the reference books in the reference section. Other students need to use them."

Brick paused, then replaced the dictionary.

Briiiiiiiiiiiiiiiiiiiing!

The bell. Alex heaved a sigh of relief. Part one: accomplished!

chapter 8

The Umpire's Card

Alex hopped onto the bus and collapsed into the seat beside Bob. Without question this had been the most stressful day of his entire life. He imagined himself being interviewed as a one-hundred-year-old man.

"Sir, you have lived over 36,500 days. What was the most stressful day of your life?"

Without hesitation, the hundred-year-old Alex answered, "The day I survived Brick Johnson."

"You mean Brick Johnson, the hardened criminal?" the reporter asked in amazement.

"I knew Brick wouldn't hurt you," Bob said in a voice that sounded a little too much like "I told you so."

"Wait a minute! Are you forgetting that Brick Johnson threatened me?"

Bob crossed his arms over his chest. "He didn't threaten to *do* anything. You said so yourself."

Alex was silent. Bob was right.

"Don't say bad things about my friends," Bob added.

Friends! Since when were Brick and Bob friends? Alex started to say something but decided against it. Bob could be really stubborn.

They rode in silence for a minute, then Bob said, "Harriet spit on me again."

"Did you show her your spit glob?" Alex asked.

"Yeah, but it fell on my shoe. She laughed at me. I wish I'd never spit on her in the first place."

"You spit on her first? No wonder she's after you," Alex said.

He thought back to that day in the cafeteria when he had done his Brick imitation. He, too, had started it, just like Bob.

"I want baseball cards tomorrow," Bob said in a small voice.

"I brought Mike Piazza to you during class."

"I know, but Mike Piazza didn't help me. I want Sid Bream."

"Sid's not playing anymore," Alex said.

"I don't care. I saw him on TV. I like him. He's nice."

"Okay, you can take Sid. I know someone else you can take, too."

"Who?"

"Roberto Alomar."

"Who's he?" Bob asked.

"He plays second base. Once he got mad and spit on an umpire."

"What did the umpire do?"

"Gave him timeout, just like Harriet," Alex said.

"I want the umpire's card. Do umpires have cards?"

"No."

"Okay, I'll take Roberto Alomar and Sid Bream."

"I'll get them as soon as we get home," Alex said.

"Thanks," Bob said. He seemed genuinely relieved.

Alex wished it was that easy for him. He leaned back in the seat and closed his eyes. One day of hiding had completely worn him out. Maybe some people, like "the Fugitive," could live like that. He could not. He thought about Walt, who was calm, relaxed, and always ready for action. Last night a student had tried to sneak up on him. Walt had whirled around and flipped the student onto the ground. Walt was like all the action heroes rolled into one—definitely cool.

Walt was wise, too. He would know exactly how to handle Brick. He might use a round kick, or he might use that slick move he used on the student who sneaked up on him. Or maybe he would do something totally different, like . . .

Alex wasn't sure what Walt would do. One thing was for sure, Walt would not hide. He would face the situation. Tomorrow, Alex would not hide. He would face the situation.

His survival now depended on one thing. Karate.

Alex imagined himself doing a smooth, powerful round kick and flattening Brick. Then he thought about Brick reading to the first graders. His desire to use his round kick faded a little. He thought about his own imitation of Brick, and his desire faded even more.

chapter 9

A Crumpled Gray Wad

Alex sat at the kitchen table and tried to finish his homework. He couldn't concentrate. In his mind he was one hundred years old again.

"Sir, which of your famous karate moves saved you from Brick Johnson?" the reporter asked.

In a dignified voice, the hundred-year-old Alex answered, "My round kick—simple yet effective."

Suddenly, the reporter blurted out, "You mean you used a round kick on Brick Johnson, that fine upstanding citizen?"

"Fine upstanding citizen?" Alex couldn't believe it. His own thoughts were betraying him.

Liz dropped a box of pizza on the table in front of him.

"I see you didn't get maimed. I guess that means I don't get your baseball cards."

Bob appeared in the doorway. "Where's Mom?" he asked.

Liz answered. "They called her in to work, some bus wreck. A bunch of people were *maaaaaaaimed.*" She looked at Alex and smiled.

"Alex didn't get maimed today," Bob said. "Brick wouldn't do that. Besides, Alex can run faster than Brick."

Liz laughed. "Do you think you can run for the rest of your life?"

Liz could spot a bad plan a mile away, and she was brutally truthful. She would have said to the little pigs, "Do you think sticks and straw will stand up to wolf-breath?"

And she would have said to the *Titanic*'s boarding passengers, "Do you plan to ride that boat through an ocean full of icebergs?"

Alex didn't mention karate. Liz would have had some snappy answer, and he didn't want to hear it.

"Baseball cards can help. Isn't that right?" Bob was saying.

"What?" Alex asked.

"Baseball cards help, don't they?" Bob said.

Liz chimed in. "Do you think baseball cards will work against flesh and blood—Brick's flesh and blood?"

"Yes," Bob said firmly.

Alex didn't answer. He knew better than to argue with Liz.

"Well, how much help will this one be?"

Liz tossed a crumpled gray wad onto the table in front of Alex. He picked up the card. The out-

line of a player's arm was still visible in the corner of the wad.

"I found it in the dryer," Liz said.

"Who is it?" Bob asked.

Alex thought back to whose card he had been carrying the day before. He had had a social studies test on Mexico so he had taken the only player he knew from Mexico.

"Fernando Valenzuela," he said meekly.

Yesterday the bright colors on the card had made Fernando look alive and powerful. Now he was a crumpled gray wad, barely visible.

Alex looked at his own bright shirt. Today he was alive and colorful. Tomorrow would he be a crumpled gray wad?

"Are you taking Ted Williams tomorrow?" Bob asked.

"No, I didn't get Ted Williams. I asked just about everybody in the whole school. Nobody had one. I called the shop downtown. They sold the last one a week ago."

"Too bad," Bob said.

"I know. I need Ted Williams."

"Who are you taking?" Bob asked.

Alex tossed the wad into the trashcan. He would not be a crumpled gray wad. Karate would save him. He thought of the flexibility needed for karate.

"I'm taking shortstops. Ozzie Smith. Derek Jeter. And Nomar Garciaparra."

chapter 10

The Flying Karate Boy

Alex felt good in his gi. He kept glancing at himself in the mirror.

Walt came over and bowed. "Glad to see you came early again. That shows commitment and discipline."

Alex liked Walt. He was the perfect sensei. That's what they called a karate instructor. Walt was always saying things like "Keep trying" or "You'll get it." And Walt said everyone was a "work in progress." Alex liked that. It meant you didn't have to be perfect.

"There's a new fifth-grade boy starting tonight. I told him to come early," Walt said.

Alex wondered who it was. He hadn't heard

anyone mention it at school. Of course, he hadn't had much time to talk. He had spent the whole day avoiding Brick Johnson.

Walt stretched his hand past Alex. "You must be Brick."

Alex wheeled around. Brick Johnson was only inches away. "This is Alex," Walt said.

Alex opened his mouth to say something, but nothing came out.

"I know Alex," Brick said, staring straight at Alex.

"Great. Then let's get started. Follow me," Walt said.

Alex walked behind Brick. He couldn't believe his terrible luck. Of all the people in his whole school, Brick Johnson had to show up. Why Brick? Deep down Alex knew. Karate was the perfect way to maim someone.

Walt stopped by the punching bag.

"Alex, why don't you show Brick the stretching exercises while I go get the forms for him to fill out."

"Wait," Alex called feebly as Walt disappeared into the office.

Alex turned to Brick. He tried to read Brick's face. There was nothing there. Brick was working his fingers in and out. They looked like ten little fat men exercising in unison.

"What are you waiting for? Let's start," Brick finally said.

Alex swallowed hard. "First, we have to stretch out our muscles. That's so you won't hurt yourself when you do your punches."

"What kind of punches?" Brick asked. The fat men quit exercising and Brick looked interested.

"Well, sometimes we use our arms, like this."

Alex punched the air a few times, yelling "*Kiai*" each time.

"And sometimes we use our legs, like this. *Kiai!*"

Brick nodded thoughtfully. Alex figured he was memorizing each punch and kick to use later.

Alex sat on the floor.

"First, we stretch. Like this."

Brick sat beside Alex and copied each move. He was very flexible, more flexible than Alex would have guessed. It looked as if he had been doing this all his life.

"You boys all stretched out?" Walt asked. He extended his hand and helped Brick up.

Brick extended his hand to Alex.

Brick looked even larger from Alex's viewpoint on the floor. Alex imagined Brick yanking him up so hard that he flew through the air and landed in a heap on the other side of the room. Alex would forever be known as "the flying karate boy."

Reluctantly, Alex took Brick's hand. Brick helped him up.

"Now let's try a few round kicks," Walt said.

Brick stood with his hands clasped behind his back, like a soldier ready to receive instructions for a battle.

"Alex, show Brick the round kick."

Alex took his position. He held his head high. He had practiced last night and again after school. Maybe the sight of his powerful round kick would scare Brick.

Alex swung his leg up and slapped the bag.

"Good," Walt said. "You practiced."

Alex smiled.

"Okay, Brick, your turn."

Without saying a word, Brick stepped up to the bag and assumed a perfect position, no wobbling.

"Good position. Now try the kick," Walt said.

Brick's face was the picture of concentration. He swung his leg up for a perfect round kick. The bag vibrated with a smack.

Walt whistled. "I'm impressed. Very good. Plenty of power."

Alex felt his confidence melt away. It had taken him hours of practice to get a good round kick. Brick had it perfect on the first try.

chapter 11

Daffy Duck Karate

Walt held the bag while Alex and Brick took turns practicing.

Alex watched Brick. Brick looked exactly like a brick, square and wide. He looked solid, too. Why in the world had he imitated this brick-looking person? He could have imitated anyone. Frankenstein. The President. Elvis. He even looked a little like Elvis. Why Brick? It had been an incredibly stupid thing to do.

"Brick, why do you want to learn karate?" Walt asked.

"I want to learn self-defense," Brick said.

That was the stupidest thing Alex had ever heard. Why would a person named Brick, who obviously had all the characteristics of a brick, need to defend himself? Only an idiot would pick on him. Alex wanted to kick himself for being that idiot. It wouldn't be necessary. Brick would do it for him, using his powerful round kick.

Walt said, "Good, Brick. Karate is the martial art of unarmed self-defense. It comes from a Japanese word meaning 'empty hand.'"

This was disgusting. Not only did Brick catch on fast, but he also knew the right answers.

Brick did a few more kicks, each one perfect.

"Have you taken karate before?" Walt asked.

"Yeah. I took some classes in Ohio before we moved here."

Alex's mouth dropped open. Brick already knew karate. No wonder he looked so natural.

"Did you do any sparring?" Walt asked.

"Yeah, some."

Brick could spar! Alex felt sick.

"Good, maybe you can show Alex a few moves," Walt said.

Alex couldn't believe this. All day Brick had

been trying to show him a few moves. Now Walt was making it easy for him to flatten Alex.

Walt turned to Alex. "I want you to do your round kick again but this time straight at Brick. Don't actually kick him. Kick in front of him."

Alex felt numb. What if he accidentally kicked Brick? Brick was already mad. Kicking him would just make him madder.

Alex was suddenly aware that he was sweating. "Are you sure?" he asked Walt.

"Go ahead," Walt said. He nodded toward Brick. "Protect yourself."

Brick assumed a solid-looking position with his arms up.

Alex took his position. A wave of nausea passed over him. He'd better hurry up before he threw up on Brick.

He took a deep breath, swung his leg forward, and delivered a perfect round kick. Suddenly, he was on the floor, staring at the ceiling.

"What happened?" he asked.

"Defense," Walt answered. "Brick blocked your

kick. He caught your leg here and pushed up. You have to watch for that."

Alex sat up. Once he had seen Daffy Duck diligently practice fencing only to be flattened with one simple move by Bugs Bunny. Now Alex knew exactly how Daffy felt.

"Good job, Brick," Walt said. He looked down at Alex. "You'll learn more about blocking in the fourth class."

Alex stared at the ceiling. The fourth class! Brick would be a black belt by then.

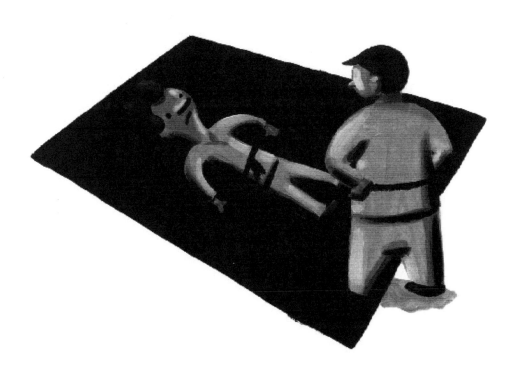

Alex tried to imagine his interview as a hundred-year-old man. It was pointless. He would never make it to one hundred.

Alex got up slowly. Brick faced him. Suddenly, Brick bowed deeply. Alex couldn't believe it. Bowing was a show of respect!

Alex bowed to Brick.

Alex thought back to the cafeteria when his mouth had been filled with food and he had done his Brick imitation. That was not respect. If only he had shown a little respect in the first place, he wouldn't be in so much trouble with Brick. Walt was right. Respect *was* harder than fighting.

chapter 12

The Braves

The ride to school was a slow one. Alex sat quietly. His heart wasn't pounding. He didn't feel nervous. In the seat next to him, Bob was shuffling his two cards, Sid Bream and Roberto Alomar. First Sid was on top. Then Roberto. Then Sid. Then Roberto. Then Sid.

"Stop shuffling the cards," Alex said.

Bob stopped. He held one card in each hand. He looked up at Alex and studied his face.

"Did you bring the shortstops with you?"

"No."

"Did you bring any cards?"

"Yes. The Braves."

"That's good," Bob said. His voice softened.

"But you won't need them. Brick isn't going to bother you. He's not like that."

Bob's picture of Brick was completely different from Alex's. Alex thought about his favorite workbook page from the first grade. It was the one where you picked out the picture that was different from the rest. There would be an apple, an orange, a bunch of grapes, and a tricycle. Alex would draw a big circle around the tricycle. He loved picking out the picture that was different.

A large activity page with pictures of Brick appeared in his mind.

1. Brick reading to first graders

2. Brick imitating dogs

3. Brick, the Braves fan

4. Brick, the bully

A big circle formed around "Brick, the bully." Maybe Brick wasn't a bully. Maybe Bob was right. At this point, it didn't matter.

Alex turned to Bob. "Have you ever thought about respect?"

"What's respect?" Bob asked.

Alex thought for a moment. He turned to Susan Green, who was sitting behind them.

"Can I borrow your dictionary?"

She handed it to him.

Alex flipped through the pages.

"R . . . e . . . s . . . Here it is. *Respect*. To honor. To show regard for."

Bob said, "I know honor. Like honor your mother and father. Make them feel special."

"That's right," Alex said.

"I like honoring, so I might like respect," Bob said.

"Bob, why don't you respect Harriet today? I know it sounds crazy, but before she has a chance to spit on you, do something nice for her."

Bob wrinkled his forehead as he considered the suggestion.

chapter 13

A Collector

Alex stepped off the bus. Whatever happened, he would take it like a man. He had seen brave men on TV. They held their heads high and marched into battle. He would display that same bravery now.

"Would you like to have Sid Bream and Roberto Alomar?" Bob asked.

"No, thanks," Alex said, touched by the gesture.

Alex pulled the Braves out of his pocket. The pitchers were on top. He looked them over for encouragement. Greg Maddux, smart. John Smoltz, determined. Tom Glavine, precise. All brave.

Alex took a deep breath. He was ready to face Brick. Without hesitation, he walked through the school door.

With his head held high, Alex passed all the likely hiding places: water fountain, boys' restroom. He expected Brick to jump out at any moment.

No Brick.

Alex walked the same hallway again, this time slower.

No Brick.

Alex stared at the almost empty hallway. This was insane. Yesterday Brick was turning up left and right all day long. Now he was nowhere to be seen. Maybe today he was sick. Impossible. He had looked perfectly healthy last night in karate class.

Alex checked his watch. 7:56. Only four minutes to get to class. He'd have to hurry to make it. He rounded the corner quickly.

Bam!

Alex bounced off a large object and hit the ground. For a moment he was stunned. He rolled over. Brick stood at the corner.

"Oh, hi, Brick. I was just looking for you," Alex said, trying to sound casual.

"Yeah. I was looking for you, too."

Alex stood up. For one awful moment he thought that his legs might start running without any command from him, like the involuntary muscles he had studied in science. He would not run anymore. He would be brave.

Alex looked at Brick. Brick's shirt was tucked in today, and he didn't look quite so big. He was wearing a Mets cap. That was no surprise. The Braves had lost last night.

Alex took a step forward.

"Go ahead," he said.

"What do you mean?" Brick asked.

Alex couldn't stand it anymore. Words poured out of his mouth. "I mean, go ahead. Do your round kick, or hit me, or maim me, or whatever. Just do it. Please. I'm an idiot."

Brick looked at Alex like he was crazy. "What are you talking about?"

"I thought you were going to . . . uh . . . do something," Alex said.

"Like what?"

"I don't know. I thought maybe . . . uh. Well . . . Then why were you looking for me?"

"I heard you needed a Ted Williams card. I have one."

Alex let out a small laugh. He threw his hand over his heart. He felt his baseball cards in his pocket. He pulled them out and kissed the top card.

"What's that?" Brick asked.

Alex looked at the top card.

"That's John Smoltz. He's a pitcher for the Bra—"

"I know who John Smoltz is. Is that a rookie card?"

"Yeah."

Brick stepped forward. "Let me see that."

Alex held the card out. Brick took the card carefully, holding it by the edges. Brick stared at the card. His face took on a look that Alex recognized. He had seen that look on the face of others who shared his passion. Brick was a collector.

"I have Tom Glavine and Greg Maddux rookie cards, too," Alex said. He fanned them out for Brick to see.

"I think I have a Greg Maddux rookie card, but I'm not sure."

"Not sure?" Alex couldn't believe it. How could anyone not be sure about something like that?

"All my cards are in a big box under my bed," Brick explained.

"They aren't organized?" Alex asked in disbe-lief. Having all those cards and not doing anything with them was like having a big bag of candy and never eating any.

Brick shrugged. "There are so many. I never got around to it. It's going to take me forever to find Ted Williams."

"You could organize them according to year, or team. You could pull out the Cy Young winners, or the All-Stars. I could help," Alex offered.

"Really?" Brick said.

"Yeah. Sit with me at lunch today and we'll make plans," Alex said.

Brick smiled.

"Can I ask you something?" Alex asked.

"I guess."

"Remember that day in the cafeteria?"

"I'm in the cafeteria every day," Brick said.

"No. That day. The day you stopped by my table."

"I don't remember."

"You have to remember. You said, 'At my other school a boy did an imitation of me and . . .'"

"And?"

"And then you stopped. And I was wondering—everyone at the table was—about what the rest of the sentence was. You have to remember. 'At my other school a boy did an imitation of me and . . .'"

"Oh, yeah. I remember. At my other school a boy did an imitation of me and his imitation was better than yours!"

"*His* was better than *mine*?" Alex burst out laughing.

"A lot better," Brick said.

"I should have done Elvis," Alex said.

Brick nodded. "You look a little like Elvis."

chapter 14

A Red Crayon
and Respect

Bob's nose was pressed against the window of the bus. His face lit up as soon as he saw Alex.

Alex hopped onto the bus and sat in the seat next to Bob.

"Brick didn't get you," Bob said.

"No. In fact, he's coming over today."

"Today?"

"Yeah, we worked it out at lunch. He called his mother from the office." Alex peered out the window and scanned the crowd for Brick.

"I knew Brick wouldn't hurt you," Bob said.

"You were right," Alex said. "Brick is no bully. I mean, think about it. I was the one who started the whole thing."

"You did? I didn't know that."

"I guess I didn't mention it. Hey, what happened with Harriet?"

"I respected her," Bob said proudly.

"What happened?"

"We were coloring pictures. Harriet needed a red crayon. Red is her favorite color, and her red crayon was all worn down. I gave her my red."

"Good. Did she spit on you?" Alex asked.

"No. She spit on Matthew."

Alex laughed.

"Maybe you can tell Matthew about respect."

"I will," Bob said. "And Harriet, too. But she likes spitting."

"Organize a spitting contest," Alex suggested.

"Good idea," Bob said.

"Hey, there's Brick," Alex said. He banged on the window and waved at Brick.

Brick climbed onto the bus and sat next to Alex and Bob.

"Are you coming to our house today?" Bob asked Brick.

"Yeah. I want to see Alex's baseball cards."

"Do you have baseball cards?" Bob asked.

"Yeah," Brick said.

Alex added, "He has some good ones—ones that belonged to his father. And he has a Ted Williams."

"I've got Sid Bream and Roberto Alomar," Bob said proudly.

"They're good," Brick said. "Sid Bream made that run for the Braves to win the 1992 National

League Championship Series." He told them how all the players piled on top of Sid Bream after he slid into home.

"Braves win! Braves win! Braves win!" Brick said, imitating the announcer.

Alex smiled. It was one of his favorite moments in baseball history.

Suddenly, Alex was a hundred years old again. The reporter was asking the final question of the interview.

"Sir, you and Brick Johnson have been friends for ninety years. Can you sum up your relationship in one word?"

"Yes, I can," Alex said. Then he paused for effect.

"Respect."